Madame Belzile and
Ramsay Hitherton-Hobbs

Budge Wilson

illustrations by
Etta Moffatt

NIMBUS
PUBLISHING

Nimbus Publishing Limited
P.O. Box 9301, Station A
Halifax, N.S.
B3K 5N5

Design Editor: Kathy Kaulbach
Project Editor: Alexa Thompson

Nimbus Publishing Limited gratefully acknowledges the support of the Maritime Council of Premiers and the Department of Communications.

Canadian Cataloguing in Publication Data

Wilson, Budge.

Madame Belzile and Ramsay Hitherton-Hobbs

(New waves)

ISBN 0-921054-38-6

I. Moffatt, Etta. II. Title. III. Series.

PS8595.I47M32 1990   jC813'.54   C90-097641-1
PZ7.W54Ma 1990

Printed and bound in Canada

*A Children's
Book Centre Choice*

To Mary Henderson
artist, friend

Contents

1
Sitting on the Veranda

Once upon a time, not very long ago, a lady sat on her veranda and watched the world go by. It was September 3. She was sixty years old, which may well seem very elderly indeed to you. But sixty is only forty years older than twenty. And twenty, as everyone knows, is exceedingly young.

The woman's name was Madame Belzile. She was called Madame instead of Mrs. because she came from Québec. All her friends and relations from there were French. When they came to visit her from Québec (which was not often) there was such a babble and clatter of talk coming from the veranda that passersby looked at the sidewalk and pretended not to hear. It made them feel nervous and embarrassed not to be able to understand what was being said.

But Madame Belzile spoke perfect English.

She had lived in Halifax, Nova Scotia, for thirty years. Almost anyone, unless they are particularly lazy, or possibly very shy, can learn a language in thirty years.

Madame Belzile was very, very thin. She was so thin that someone once heard old Mr. Harrison say that you could shoot peas through her. She had beautiful thick brown hair and enormous black eyes, but that seemed to be all she had to offer. The rest of her was so scrawny that her skin was like paper stretched over bones. Behind her back, people called her Madame Pipe Cleaner. (If you have ever seen a pipe cleaner, you will understand why they chose this name for her.)

Madame Belzile was not a happy person. Probably this was the reason she was so thin. If you are very unhappy, usually you do one of two things: either you eat too much, or you eat too little. Madame Belzile ate too little—a cup of black coffee for breakfast, an egg for lunch, with two small crackers, half a sandwich made of Spam and lettuce for supper. You can't get very fat on *that*. If she had had her choice,

Madame Belzile would have existed entirely on black coffee, in which case she probably would not have existed for very long. But she was well aware of that fact. Therefore she forced herself to eat the egg, the crackers, and the sandwich every single day.

Madame Belzile was sad because she was lonely. Her three beautiful daughters were grown up and married. She would have liked them to live in Halifax, or even in Truro, which is only one hundred kilometres away. But they lived in Australia and Alaska and France. Can you believe such bad luck? She even had grandchildren, but grandchildren are almost entirely useless if they are too far away to be seen or talked to.

What's more, Madame's husband, Monsieur Gaston Belzile, had died five years ago of a heart attack. Before he died, she had found the way he chewed on his front teeth, and left his shoes lying around for her to trip over, very irritating. Also, the way he bit his nails—*out loud*—got on her nerves. But now that he was dead, she never thought about those things.

Instead, she remembered the way he called her "*ma petite poupée*," which means "my little doll." Certainly, no one called her that any more. She also recalled the way he had praised her for her wonderful meals—for her *coq au vin*, her *escargots au gratin*, her light and fluffy *tartes aux pommes* (all eaten, of course, with his front teeth). And she often thought about the way, after each meal, he kissed her on the back of her neck and said, "*Merci, ma belle petite fille.*" This means "Thank you, my beautiful little girl," and by the time you are nearly sixty years old, only a husband is apt to say such a lovely thing.

She could remember more good things about him. Every once in a while—for no apparent reason—he would say, "*Tu es ma meilleure amie.*" It is nice to hear someone say, right out of the blue, that you are his best friend—particularly if that person happens to be your husband. Monsieur Belzile hadn't been dead half an hour before she realized that he had been *her* best friend, too. But *hélas!* Alas! It was too late to tell him that.

So now Madame Belzile was all alone. Her best friend had died, and her second-best friend had moved back to Québec City. After all those disasters, she discovered that she didn't have the courage to call up her third-best friend to ask her over for tea.

Madame Belzile was not just alone and lonely. She also had no one to speak to in French. It is true that she could speak English beautifully, but once in a while, she had a deep yearning to speak French. It was like wanting a drink of water when you are thirsty—or like longing to see the sea if you are a native Newfoundlander living on the Sahara Desert. It was a little nagging thing just under her ribs that prevented her from feeling one hundred percent at peace most of the time.

2
Ramsay Moves In

Down the block from Madame Belzile—three houses away, to be exact—a moving van stopped, ground its gears into reverse, and backed into the driveway. Madame Belzile leaned over her veranda railing and watched as three men and a lot of furniture started spilling out of the truck. One by one, the men carried out sofas, a green piano (green!), long rolls of carpeting, cardboard cartons by the dozen, a bicycle, two television sets, and an immense dining-room table.

Madame Belzile could learn nothing from this collection of furniture. The green piano might mean that her new neighbors were musical. On the other hand, some people keep pianos just for decoration (particularly green ones). She couldn't imagine why any family would need two television sets. And anyone can ride a bicycle. She hoped that there would be children, particularly little girls. She was used to little girls. If children weren't too noisy and if they didn't pick your tulips, they could be interesting to watch.

Most of all, Madame Belzile wanted the family to be able to speak French. But this was just a tiny little wish, which couldn't even be described as a hope. When the men had emptied the truck, they drove away. The family had not arrived yet.

The next day, Madame Belzile rose at 7:00 a.m. (two hours and a half before her usual time) and put on her best yellow dress —because *you just never know*. The family might speak French, and, if they did, she wanted to be looking her best. She had her cup of black coffee and settled down on the veranda to wait.

When the family drove up in an enormous shiny black car, there were only three people in it. As they turned into the driveway, she

could see their heads well enough to count them. When the car door opened, a woman stepped out—very tall, very dignified, dressed in a navy-blue suit with a white blouse. Then came the man—very tall, very dignified, dressed in a navy-blue suit with a white shirt and a maroon tie. At last a little boy came out—very short, very fat, very solemn, dressed in a pair of navy-blue overalls with a white T-shirt. They talked quietly to one another, and then disappeared inside the house.

Madame Belzile felt her heart go *thud* inside her chest. There was no little girl to push a doll carriage up and down the sidewalk. And the little boy looked much too serious and much too fat. Worst of all, this absolutely could not be a Francophone family. They were far too serious, much too quiet, and there were no smiles. Madame Belzile did not give any thought at all to the fact that for five whole years, she had been very serious, very quiet and almost never smiled. She went inside and took off her yellow dress. She skipped lunch and had a nap instead.

At five o'clock, she was wakened by the doorbell. Putting on her red housecoat, the one with the mauve pansies all over it, she opened the front door. There he was—the new, little fat boy.

"My name is Ramsay," he said. "My last name is Hitherton-Hobbs."

Madame Belzile's heart sank a little lower. She had, after all, continued to harbor a hope—or at least a wish. No one called Ramsay Hitherton-Hobbs could possibly be Francophone. But she had better say something to this solemn child. The little boy's eyes were large and curious, and he appeared to be astonished.

"How do you do," she said with typical French courtesy, and held out her hand. He shook it. He was only nine years old, but he knew what to do with an outstretched hand. "My name is Madame Belzile," she said. "May I help you?"

"Yes," he replied, "or at least I hope so. It's almost supper time, and my mother can't find the can opener. She doesn't cook," he explained.

"She works. She has a very important job. So does my father. He works, too. It's Sunday, and all the stores are closed. Do you have a can opener?"

Madame Belzile fetched a can opener. She also took out of the freezer a large *tourtière*, which she'd been keeping for the annual visit of her brother-in-law's sister from Chicoutimi.

"Thank you very much," said Ramsay, bowing ever so slightly. "This looks like other people's food."

Madame Belzile listened to the way he spoke. Maybe he was from England. She couldn't tell for sure.

But he didn't leave. He was just standing there looking at her. "Yes?" she inquired. "More problems?"

"I just wanted to tell you that you are very, very beautiful," he said, eyes aglitter. "I have never ever seen anyone so lovely and skinny. Perhaps you could tell me how you got that way."

She considered being insulted for a moment but realized almost at once that she had received a compliment. "Thank you," she said. "I'm glad you like it—the skinniness, that is. Not everyone would share your point of view. But to answer your question: you get that way by being sad and having no appetite."

He sighed. He didn't say anything else. He just turned and waddled away.

3
Ramsay's First Day at School

The next day, Madame Belzile was sitting on her veranda (which she called a balcony) when Ramsay returned from his first day at school.

"Hello," she said. "Did you like your new school?"

"No," he replied.

"Why?"

He came over and carefully lowered himself onto her front step. His stomach was bulging over his jeans, and his arms had fat rings around the wrists, like a baby's.

"They called me Fatso," he said in a voice she could barely hear. "Melody Hennigar sits behind me. She started it. She called me Fatso *three times*." He sighed. "And the work's really scary. The math is harder than anything I ever did. And they have *French* in this awful school. I haven't had *that* before. What a drag! So now I'm fat *and* stupid." He buried his head in his hands. Then he added, "That Melody Hennigar said 'hi' to me when I first came in. She even smiled. But she's so pretty that my tongue sort of seized up and I didn't answer her."

Madame Belzile didn't know what to do. She wanted to put her scrawny arms around him and give him a big hug, but even the French do not do this on the very first day after meeting someone.

"Maybe your mother can help you feel better," she suggested. "Mothers are good at that. So are fathers, when they get home."

Ramsay sighed again.

"Well?" she asked.

"Well nothing," he said, adjusting his bulk to a more comfortable position. "I told you. She works. So does he. When they get home, it's six o'clock and cranky time—and can openers or restaurants. Then they want peace. That's what they say. I wish I had a brother—or even a sister."

"What do your parents do for a living?" asked Madame Belzile, knowing she was being nosey. But she was feeling cross at these parents, so, for a moment, she forgot her lifelong habit of being polite.

"She's a big computer expert," he replied, "and he's a big important business man. He does his business all over the world. We move a lot; but that's no excuse, is it?"

"For what?" asked Madame Belzile, thinking of how much it must cost to move that green piano all over the world.

"For being tired every evening—for always wanting it to be peaceful—for not giving me any brothers or sisters." He kicked the side of the step, but because he was so fat, his foot just went *thunk* instead of *crack*.

Madame Belzile was nodding her head up and down. But she also wanted to be fair. "You can't always control some of those things," she said.

Ramsay pretended that he hadn't heard her. "My mother said to thank you for the meat pie," he said.

Meat pie! A *tourtière* is a *tourtière*. But she must try to be broad-minded, so she spoke softly. "That was a *tourtière*. It's *special*. It's made of many, many ingredients, and you have to cook it for *four hours*." Then she added, "I'm sorry you're sad. It's sad to be sad."

He looked at her as though he might like to say something else, but then he said abruptly, "Gotta go. I'm hungry. Gotta eat."

Madame Belzile was on the point of asking him if he would like a cookie but, by the time she got started on her invitation, he was gone.

4
Madame Belzile Has an Idea

The next day, when Ramsay Hitherton-Hobbs came trudging home from school, Madame Belzile was ready. She had on her yellow dress, and she was sitting in her rocking chair on her veranda.

"So," she inquired, as he passed the house, "any better?"

He stopped. His little fat face was a very sad sight indeed. "Worse," he said. "Tubby, Fat-stuff, Hippo—those are just *some* of the names. And it's not just from Melody Hennigar—the freckle-faced boy has started doing it, too. How would *you* like that? Oh, how I'd love to have your arms—just like sticks! And the math gets worse and worse. But *nothing's* as terrible as that disgusting old French. I don't know one single word, and they laugh and laugh when I try. I wish I knew Italian or something so I could amaze them. *I want so badly to amaze them.* I hate them all. I wish I was dead—or at the North Pole—or somewhere a billion miles away."

He just stood there. His face wasn't screwed up or anything, but big tears were running down his fat cheeks.

"I'm going home to eat," he said, "till supper time."

That did it. Madame Belzile knew that Ramsay Hitherton-Hobbs wasn't her child, and that the whole thing was none of her business—but she had made up her mind.

"Oh no, you're not!" she said, rising from her chair so that he could enjoy the full benefit of her yellow dress. "I can't do one single thing about the math, but I think that, between us, we can fix up everything else. Come up on the balcony and sit in the sun. I'll bring out a little table. Then we'll both have a glass of skim milk and our first French lesson. This is to be a very big secret between you and me. You want to amaze them? *You will.*"

Ramsay looked up at her from his perch on the steps. He looked at her yellow dress and thought it was very pretty indeed. And it was pleasant to be in the company of anyone who was that thin. The scalloped sleeves on the dress made her arms look even skinnier. The full skirt made her legs seem all the more wonderful; they emerged from the fullness like two long mop handles.

Ramsay was so delighted, that for a moment he forgot his own worries. He didn't believe a thing she was telling him about amazing his classmates, but he liked having someone to talk to and he liked being here.

"Thanks," he said. "Don't mind if I do."

Ramsay followed her inside the house and helped her with the chair and table. It was hard for anyone that fat to carry a chair, but he managed to do it without tripping or falling or doing any other embarrassing thing. But he did it to the accompaniment of a lot of heavy breathing.

Madame Belzile put a little lace cloth on the

table and two small plates. Finally, she gave him a saucer of cheese slices to take out, and six small crackers. She brought two green napkins and two glasses of skim milk. Then they sat down.

"Three slices of cheese for you," she said, "and three crackers. *Et la même chose pour moi.*" He couldn't understand the words that she was saying, but he knew what she meant. He piled the three crackers and three cheese slices on his plate immediately—in case she might get mixed up with her own counting. If there were to be no cookies or cakes or doughnuts or chocolate bars or chips or large bottles of pop, he'd better be sure he at least got what was coming to him. The skim milk looked blue and tasted blue. He ate and drank everything quickly, and then sat back to look at Madame Belzile, his hands folded across his stomach. He felt as though he might be starving to death.

"*Eh bien ...*" she began.

"Miss Kinsett knows how to say that, too," he said, his voice low and dreary. "She's our French teacher."

"Well," she said. "It's not very hard to say. Try it. *Eh bien.*"

"*Eh bien,*" he said.

"Marvellous! *Magnifique! Formidable!*" she exclaimed. "It means 'Well now …' or sort of. It's just a way of getting started with something you're going to say."

"Which is?" asked Ramsay, wondering how soon he could leave this house and get home to his mother's cookie jar.

"*Eh bien,*" she began again, "I thought I'd like to teach you some French every single day. They can't know all *that* much in Grade 4. *Pas beaucoup.* Not very much at all. I'm sure I could teach you all that in a couple of months."

A couple of months! That seemed a long time. Would that mean skim milk and crackers for two whole months? Eight weeks … and eight times seven days … a long time. Still …

Madame Belzile was speaking. "By the end of October, even before the leaves fall, you could be as good in French as anyone in your class." She paused. "Besides," she said shyly, wistfully, "it's a very beautiful language."

"Huh!" snorted Ramsay. "I'd like to believe *that!* But ..."

"But what?" prompted Madame Belzile, trying to forget his other statement.

Ramsay thought some more. With bad math marks, no French, a fat body, and with kids yattering at him in the schoolyard, he didn't have much choice. There had to be *something* good in his life.

"Just *but*." He sighed. "OK. Let's do it." He took a deep breath. "When do we start?"

"Right this minute," said Madame Belzile. "*Immédiatement*." She put down her napkin. "*La serviette*," she said, pointing to it. "Just like in English."

"*La serviette*," repeated Ramsay.

"*Moi*," she said, pointing to herself.

"*Moi*," he said, poking his thumb into his own chest.

"*Toi*," she said, pointing to him.

"*Toi*," he repeated, grinning and pointing to her.

"*Nous deux ensemble*," she said. "You and me together. That's how it's going to be until we can amaze them. Now, try this: '*J'aime parler français.*'"

"*J'aime parler français,*" repeated Ramsay.

Madame Belzile smiled. "Oh, I hope so, Ramsay," she sighed. "I do hope so. *J'espère que oui.*"

Then she stood up. "Enough for the first day," she announced. "Come tomorrow at the same time." She put her hand on Ramsay's fat shoulder. "Everything's going to be fine," she said. "You're going to amaze them."

5
Le Nouveau Régime

Over the next ten months, things changed a great deal for Madame Belzile and Ramsay Hitherton-Hobbs. It would be difficult to say who had to do the most changing. But, certainly, it all started with Madame Belzile. Each morning she rose at seven-thirty instead of nine-thirty. Even during the warm fall days, she did not spend her entire morning or afternoon sitting on her veranda looking pitiful. She did not have the time. She had food to prepare for Ramsay's afternoon snack—healthy, non-fattening things.

She also had French lessons to organize and plan. She went to the Public Library and read up on diets and obesity, and on matters such as "motivation" and "feelings of self-worth." She knew without being told that motivation has to do with wanting something enough to try to get it. She knew that feelings of self-worth have to do with feeling good about who you are. But she felt she needed to know more about those things if she were going to be able to help Ramsay. Little by little, she learned a whole lot. But it didn't happen all at once. Things don't change *that* fast, even when you're sixty years old.

During the second week of what she referred to as *Le Nouveau Régime*, Madame Belzile discovered that Ramsay took his lunch to school with him each day. The school was two kilometres away, and anyway, his mother was never home at noon.

One day, Madame Belzile sneaked a peek inside his lunch box. It contained four peanut-butter-and-jelly sandwiches, two candy bars, five chocolate-marshmallow cookies, two packages of potato chips, a bag of jelly beans, and a carton of chocolate milk. She fixed Ramsay with a fierce look and told him that he had *absolument* no choice: he was to come to her house every day, *tous les jours*, for lunch. If he walked very quickly, he could make it in plenty of time. *She* would prepare his lunch.

No wonder Madame Belzile had to rise at 7:30 a.m. Each morning she had to think of something that would fill Ramsay up without making him fat. Then she had to prepare it. She discovered that this took so much imagination and energy that she needed something more than black coffee for breakfast. All that thinking was exhausting. She added three rashers of bacon and a thick slice of whole-wheat toast—with a large dollop of butter.

At first, Ramsay was not sure that telling his troubles to Madame Belzile had been a very smart move. For the first two or three weeks, he was a wreck. He was starved. Every time his mind slid into neutral, (when it was not occupied, for instance, with thoughts of school or name-calling or mathematical problems or can openers) he thought about food. Technicolor visions of food floated before his mind's eye—mocha cakes, ice-cream sundaes topped with luminous red cherries, lemon meringue pie. At such moments, he thought about Madame Belzile with a great deal of anger and a lot of regret. How had he got

himself into this awful trap? His own house—empty of people, but filled with food—looked a good deal more attractive to him than it had on September 5.

But cheating was out of the question, although Ramsay certainly gave it some serious thought. The fact was that when Ramsay arrived for lunch every day, the same thing happened. Before Madame Belzile so much as said *"bonjour"* or *"comment ça va"* or "how was your day,"she *weighed* him. Then she wrote down the result on a chart on the refrigerator.

So, even when Madame Belzile was upstairs going to the washroom or looking for a diet list, Ramsay couldn't ever try to steal anything out of the refrigerator without that chart staring him in the face. Actually, one day he put his hand over the chart and opened the door. He might as well not have bothered. Inside there were two heads of lettuce, some celery sticks, a box of eggs, a bunch of parsley, a litre of skim milk, and three tomatoes. No chocolate-covered marshmallow cookies. No chips. No pop.

"Vide!" he exclaimed, without even thinking

what he was saying. *Vide* is the French word for "empty." He looked it up in the dictionary just to make sure he'd said what he meant. He had.

At noon, when Ramsay would arrive panting from his fast journey from school, his lunch would be waiting. He had to admit that there was plenty of food, even if it wasn't at all what he wanted to eat. There might be a steaming hot bowl of homemade chicken or beef soup, made from real chicken or beef bones and containing lots of fresh vegetables—carrots, peas, cabbage. There would always be a wooden bowlful of crisp lettuce or spinach, sprinkled with grated cheese. There would be a slice of some kind of meat, and a glass of skim milk—and an apple for recess.

One day, Ramsay looked at all that food, and growled, "This is so much stuff. I'm gonna go right on being fat if I eat all this. So why can't I just have a bowl of chocolate bars and a plate of cookies and a glass of chocolate milk, instead of all this dumb soup and lettuce and skim milk?"

Madame Belzile remembered what she had learned at the library, and explained things to him as simply as she could. "My dumb soup and salad and skim milk will make you grow, and make you strong, and give you lots of wonderful energy. Chocolate bars can't do all that for you."

Ramsay still couldn't get to first base fast enough for anyone to want him on the baseball team. He just didn't have enough strength to move that quickly. The freckle-faced boy was team captain, and he'd never once asked Ramsay to play. Ramsay thought about this. Then he ate up his soup and meat and tried to forget what chocolate bars tasted like.

Madame Belzile would always ask him about his day. She would also say some things in French, useful things, courteous things, such as *merci* and *s'il vous plaît* and *excusez-moi*. Or just cheerful, conversational things such as *quelle belle journée!* or *ça me fait grand plaisir de te voir*. This means "It gives me great pleasure to see you." By that time, he knew what she was saying, and he was starting to agree with her.

6
French Lessons

Madame Belzile, being from Québec and almost always unfailingly polite, knew that she could not expect Ramsay to sit and eat his lunch all by himself. She also knew that it would be a while before her kind of food appealed to him. (Had she not, after all, spent several years disliking *every* form of food?) So she tried to make the meal attractive in other ways.

When she discovered that Ramsay liked blue, she started to use her best blue tablecloth. It was permanent press so, even if he spilt *soupe aux pois* all over it, she could wash it each evening. During the warm fall days, she wore *sa robe jaune*, her yellow dress, often, because it went well with the blue. As long as the garden produced blossoms, she put a flower in a vase and placed it in the centre of the table. Then she sat down on the other side of the table and ate everything that Ramsay Hitherton-Hobbs was eating. *"Bon appétit,"* she would say to him, discovering that her own appetite was also surprisingly good.

In the afternoons, after school, the French lessons began. Madame Belzile looked up details of the Grade 4 curriculum from the schoolboard. In no time at all—much less than two months in fact—it was possible to teach Ramsay enough grammar and vocabulary to put him on a level with his classmates.

However, Madame Belzile remembered Ramsay saying that he wanted to *amaze* them. She was determined to make this possible. And so was he.

Together they agreed that he would work himself to death, if necessary, in order to be able to speak French as well as his teacher by the end of the school year. After all, she was from Lower Sackville and had learned her French in university. Ramsay was going to learn French from a real, live Québecoise, and he was going to learn to speak like one.

But he didn't know how soon he would start *thinking* in French. One morning he woke up and said to himself, right out loud, "*Il me faut brosser les dents.*" Then he went into the bathroom and brushed them.

Madame Belzile's years of twenty-four-hour-a-day sadness had not affected her intelligence. She was smart enough to know that even a much-reduced Ramsay might tire of French lessons if they were boring or too difficult. They had to be fun. Therefore, when she wasn't busy reading at the Public Library about food or children, or preparing healthy and attractive meals, she was planning French lessons of such liveliness and fun that they seemed more like games than work.

If fact, they did play games. They played Scrabble, using French words. They made up their own French crossword puzzles. And once in a long while, if Ramsay was really tired and cranky, they played checkers. Then they didn't have to speak at all.

Once a month, they had a Topsy-Turvy Day when Madame Belzile would become Ramsay, and Ramsay would become Madame Belzile. Then they would try to talk together in French. Sometimes this made them laugh so much that it was hard to speak in *any* language.

They did other things, too. They made up their own riddles, wrote poems, planned menus for the next day, argued about food. If Ramsay found carrots boring that week, he might say, *"Les carottes sont ennuyantes."*

Madame Belzile told Ramsay about her

daughters, and Ramsay told Madame Belzile about school. Madame Belzile told him about Québec City, where she'd lived when she was young. She told him about the high hills and crooked streets, about the artists spreading their paintings out on the sidewalk, about everyone laughing and singing outside the cafés in the

summertime. She told him that sometimes people even danced *on the tables*. Ramsay told her how badly he wanted to go there and see it all for himself.

And more and more, little by little, they did these things entirely in French. Madame Belzile developed into a teacher of remarkable imagination and skill.

7
Amazing Them

By now you will have guessed almost everything that eventually happened. Little by little, just as though air were being let out of a tire, Ramsay shrank. He started to walk instead of waddle. His wrists appeared, distinct bones, above his hands. The number of his chins decreased until there was just one. As fall turned into winter and then into spring, a whole new Ramsay emerged from that heap of jiggling flesh. *Il est devenu un beau garçon.* The name-calling stopped; there is no point in yelling 'Fatso' at someone who is no longer fat. By June 28, the last day of school, Ramsay looked in his mother's full-length mirror and liked what he saw.

Ramsay put on his new jeans and his favorite

Expos T-shirt, and set off for school. He walked straight and tall, and sniffed the warm air happily. Sometimes he ran for awhile and jumped over things, just because he felt like it.

The freckle-faced boy watched him from across the street, and then yelled out, "Hey! You run real fast. Wanna join the baseball team?"

"Sure!" called Ramsay.

When Ramsay met Melody Hennigar in the schoolyard, he grinned and said hi. She grinned and said hi right back. Suddenly, he knew that if he had spoken to her from the beginning, she might never have started calling him names. But it was too late to worry about that any more.

He reached his home room at school, waited through the National Anthem, the handing out of marks and report cards, and the tidying up of the classroom. He wished it would hurry up and be the last period, when Miss Kinsett would come in to say goodbye to the class.

Finally, Miss Kinsett arrived at the door. As soon as she had said her last words to the class, Ramsay stood up. Then he delivered to her—in French—a seven-minute speech of thanks and

good wishes and farewell—at least it seemed to be seven minutes long, though maybe it was only three, or even two.

To be absolutely honest, Miss Kinsett understood only about half of what he was saying. Her university courses had not prepared her for such fluency. The class listened, stunned into silence, truly *amazed*. Under the circumstances, it was no longer of interest to them that his marks in math were still the lowest in the class.

In the meantime, Madame Belzile noted that June 28 was the first really warm day of summer. It had been an uncommonly chilly spring. She pulled her favorite yellow dress out of the closet to put it on. Her trips to the Public Library had interested her in many new matters, and she was to attend a lecture that afternoon on "The Environmental Problems of the Atlantic Coast." She wanted to look nice. However, the dress would go over her head, but no further. The zipper most certainly could not be expected to zip. Heartbroken at first— because it really was a pretty dress—she was then delighted. She, too, looked at herself in a full-length mirror.

There she was, still slender, but no longer scrawny. Her skin looked like skin instead of rice paper, and there were a few little curves in places where curves look nice. The worry marks between her eyes had eased away, and what Madame Belzile was seeing was a cheerful, attractive woman with thick brown hair, a pair of beautiful eyes, and a lovely smile. For she was smiling into the mirror. Madame Belzile was smiling at Madame Belzile.

8
La Belle Province

The next day, Madame Belzile left the house to go downtown to buy a new dress. In her heart, she'd already let go of her beloved yellow dress and she was eager to look for something to take its place. Maybe she'd worn yellow long enough. A different color might be fun to try—blue, perhaps. Then, when she'd come home from the store, perhaps she'd call up that nice Stedwell woman whom she'd met at the lecture series—the one who wore her hair straight and had such a friendly smile. She might even ask her over for tea. Or perhaps she could telephone her old friend, Janine Cormier, the third-best friend whom she'd dropped like a hot potato during her long period of grief. Madame Belzile's face looked soft and hopeful as she walked along. Then she met Ramsay.

"I have news for you! *J'ai des nouvelles pour*

toi!" He grinned. *"Demain,* tomorrow, we're going—*mes parents et moi*—to Québec City, for a holiday. My parents think I should try out my French on the Québcois. They seem to think I'm gonna amaze the whole of *La Belle Province!*"

Madame Belzile felt her chest grow tight and full when she heard this wonderful news. "And how do *you* feel about it, Ramsay?" she asked.

"I can hardly wait!" breathed Ramsay.

Madame Belzile and Ramsay looked at one another with satisfaction and a great deal of love. There seemed to be very little more to say.

"Goodbye, Ramsay," said Madame Belzile.

"Au revoir, Madame Belzile," said Ramsay.

"I'll be seeing you," said Madame Belzile.

"A bientôt," said Ramsay.

They shook hands very warmly, and Madame Belzile bent down to kiss him on the top of his head. Then they remembered one more thing that needed to be said.

"Thank you very much, Ramsay," said Madame Belzile.

"Merci beaucoup, ma chère amie," said Ramsay Hitherton-Hobbs.